Asian Children's Favorite Stories

Asian Children's Favorite Stories

retold by **David Conger, Kay Lyons, Liana Romulo, Joan Suyenaga** and **Marian Davies Toth**

illustrations by **Patrick Yee**

edited by **Liana Romulo**

TUTTLE PUBLISHING
Tokyo • Rutland, Vermont • Singapore

Published by Tuttle Publishing,
an imprint of Periplus Editions (HK) Ltd,
with editorial offices at 364 Innovation Drive,
North Clarendon, VT 05759-9436, USA and
130 Joo Seng Road #06-01, Singapore 368357

Text © 2006 Periplus Editions (HK) Ltd
Illustrations © 2006 Patrick Yee
LCC Card No: 2006905342
ISBN 13: 978-0-8048-3669-2
ISBN 10: 0-0-8048-3669-8

First printing, 2006

Printed in Singapore

10 09 08 07 06
5 4 3 2 1

DISTRIBUTED BY:

North America, Latin America & Europe
Tuttle Publishing,
364 Innovation Drive,
North Clarendon, VT 05759-9436, USA
Tel: 1 (802) 773 8930 Fax: 1 (802) 773 6993
Email: info@tuttlepublishing.com
Website: www.tuttlepublishing.com

Asia Pacific
Berkeley Books Pte Ltd,
130 Joo Seng Road #06-01,
Singapore 368357
Tel: (65) 6280 1330 Fax: (65) 6280 6290
Email: inquiries@periplus.com.sg
Website: www.periplus.com

Japan
Tuttle Publishing,
Yaekari Building 3F, 5-4-12 Osaki,
Shinagawa-ku, Tokyo 141-0032
Tel: (03) 5437 0171 Fax: (03) 5437 0755
Email: tuttle-sales@gol.com

Contents

The Waters of Olive Lake
❧ China ❧

Liu had worked the fields every day, from sunup to sundown, since he was a little boy. He and his mother planted cabbages, turnips, peas, and other vegetables, yet they never seemed to have enough to eat. They lived in a tiny one-room shack, which creaked and shook violently whenever the wind blew.

Liu, who had grown up to be a selfless and compassionate man, wanted very much for his mother to retire from the hard life of farming. On cold winter mornings, he noticed that it took her a long time to get out of bed. He also dreamed of the day that he'd bring home a big piece of meat for their supper. As it was, they never had anything but vegetables and broth. Although they lived near a lake, it wasn't one that seemed to have any fish in it. Olive Lake, in fact, looked rather filthy. Its smell was so disgusting, Liu could never linger long enough to drop a line in it.

One day, when his mother appeared to be particularly weak and hungry, Liu paused from his work and sat down to think. *Why do we work so hard yet stay so poor?* he wondered.

Hours later, he was still pondering the same disturbing question. Long after the sun went down, Liu finally decided that he would visit Ru Shou, the God of the West. He wanted some answers.

Liu journeyed west on foot for many days. Then, one damp gray morning, he came across a small house along the road. Tired and weak from starvation, Liu peered into the house through a hole in a wall. He saw a beautiful young woman and an older one, who seemed to be her mother. Both were eating from large bowls billowing with steam.

The older woman looked up just as Liu was licking his lips. She then came outside and invited him in to eat. Rice porridge had never tasted so good to Liu before!

As she ladled another helping into his bowl, the woman asked Liu where he was going.

"I'm on my way to see Ru Shou," Liu said. "I'm going to ask him why I work so hard yet stay so poor."

After a moment of silence, the woman looked at him earnestly. "I have a daughter who is eighteen years old," she said, "but she has never spoken a word in her life. Could you ask him why this is so?"

"Yes, I will ask him," Liu replied simply. He stayed at the woman's house that night, and the next day set off again.

After traveling ten more days, Liu stopped at another house along his path. The kind man who lived there offered Liu food and shelter for the night.

"I hope you rest well here," the man said, showing Liu into a barn and giving him a blanket. "You have traveled quite a distance. Where are you going?"

"I'm going to see Ru Shou," Liu explained, "to find out why I work so hard yet stay so poor."

The man's eyes brightened. "I have a question for the god, too," he said, "but I cannot leave the animals long enough to go see him myself. Perhaps you could ask him for me."

Liu nodded. "Of course," he said. "You have been very kind to me."

"I have an orange tree in my garden," said the man. "It is beautiful to look at, but it never bears fruit." He opened the barn door a little wider, as if to show Liu the tree. "Please ask the god why."

Liu said goodbye to the man and started off again early the next morning.

Several days later, just when he thought he could no longer go on because he was so tired, he glimpsed an enormous structure just beyond the horizon. *Could that be Ru Shou's palace?* he wondered, shielding his eyes against the late-afternoon sun. *Oh! It is! It is!* Hope and excitement immediately sprang up inside him.

But between Liu and the palace was a river that was flowing so rapidly, its roar was deafening. *How can I possibly cross this river?* he thought, knowing full well he couldn't swim.

Liu eventually got up the courage to make his way closer to the river's edge. Just then, a huge dragon rose up out of the water, its giant teeth flashing in the waning light. Liu screamed and fell backward onto the ground. He struggled to get away as fast as he could.

"Wait!" the dragon called after him. "I'm not going to hurt you."

The dragon's voice sounded calm and gentle. Liu turned back and looked at it uncertainly.

"I just want to help you cross the river," said the dragon, lowering its head so that Liu could climb onto its neck.

Liu swallowed hard before climbing onto the dragon. "Thank you," he said loudly, so that he could be heard above the raging river. "I am trying to reach the palace on the other side of this river."

"You are going to see the god Ru Shou," the dragon said,
lowering Liu to the ground on the other side of the river.

"I would like to ask him something, but since you're going, maybe
you could do it for me."

Liu smiled, happy to help the kind dragon. "Yes. What is it?"

"I always do good things for people," the dragon began, "but I never rise up to
heaven. I want to know why."

At last Liu arrived at the gates of the palace, and received permission to
proceed to the throne room. Seated on the throne was a kind-looking old man
dressed in robes of embroidered silk. "I am the God of the West," said the man.

"Why have you come to see me?"

"I have come to ask you four questions," answered Liu.

"Four questions are forbidden," said Ru Shou. "You may ask only an odd number of questions: One and not two," he said, raising a finger. "Or you may ask three questions, but not four. Or, if you wish, you may ask five"—he shook his head— "but not six."

Liu cocked his head, puzzled. Gods always had funny rules like that, it seemed to him, but he knew it was best to just follow along. First he asked about the woman's speechless daughter. Then he went on to ask about the man's orange tree. Finally—having only one question left—he asked about why the dragon never seemed to make it to heaven.

Ru Shou graciously answered all three questions, and Liu thanked him. He figured he could always come back to ask his own question, as he was young and strong enough to make the journey again.

Once he got back to the river, he met the dragon.

"Ru Shou says you have to do two good things before you can rise up to heaven," Liu explained. "First you have to take me across the river. Then you have to take off that giant pearl on your forehead."

Upon hearing this, the dragon quickly carried Liu across the river and plucked the pearl from its forehead. Much to Liu's amazement, the large beast immediately began to rise up to heaven. As it did, the pearl dropped straight down to Liu, who caught it.

Liu traveled on until he came to the house of the man with the barren tree. "Ru Shou says there are nine jars of gold and nine jars of silver buried under your orange tree," said Liu. "Dig them up and the tree will bear fruit."

Liu had barely uttered these words when the man got down on his knees and started digging. Sure enough, he pulled from the earth nine jars of gold and nine jars of silver. As soon as he did, fruit sprang forth from the branches, as if by magic. As a reward, he gave Liu some of the gold and silver, and a few oranges to eat along the way. Liu was very happy and thanked the man. He continued on his journey, arriving at the woman's house several days later.

Liu told the woman, "Ru Shou believes your daughter will speak once she sets her eyes upon the man she is to marry."

Just then the woman's daughter walked into the room. She looked at Liu for a long time, and then she spoke. "Who is this, Mother?"

The woman was so happy to hear her daughter's voice that she immediately agreed to let Liu have her hand in marriage. So Liu once again went on his way, now even happier than before because he had with him his new wife, Ling.

At last he reached his home by the shores of Olive Lake. His mother cried with happiness when she saw him and met Ling. She was overjoyed when he showed her the precious gifts he brought with him: the gold and silver, the oranges, and the giant pearl.

"Everything would be just perfect," said Liu, caressing the luminous pearl in his palm, "if only the waters of Olive Lake would come back to life." He looked at the lake's stagnant black waters, trying not to breathe in its stinky fumes.

As soon as he spoke these words, the lake began to transform before his eyes, turning from inky blackness to crystalline clearness. Liu, his mother, and Ling all rushed to the lake's edge in amazement. How was it possible?

"That pearl," Liu's mother said, as the lake came alive with hundreds of wiggling fish, "that pearl is magical. It just granted your wish!"

Ling, Liu, and his mother had all they needed from that moment forward, and Liu never again had to wonder why he worked so hard yet stayed so poor.

Why Cats and Dogs Don't Get Along
✤ Korean ✤

Some creatures never seem to get along. But this wasn't always the case when it came to cats and dogs: a long time ago, they lived together as friends. This changed forever when a man named Shu saw his luck take a turn for the worse.

"Mmmmm," said Shu, holding a fistful of gleaming white rice to his nose. "Your rice smells absolutely heavenly!"

The farmer smiled. "Thank you," he said appreciatively. "I assure you it smells even better once it's cooked. Like perfume!" Pushing a hand into his oxcart until rice was up to his elbow, he pulled out a handful of it. The polished white grains sifted through his hand as he spoke. "So would you like to buy some?"

Shu shook his head. "Oh, no," he said. "I, too, sell rice, and I have more than enough for me and my two pets. But thank you for stopping by."

True enough, Shu always had piles of rice (and a fine variety, too), from which he made comfortable living. He and his pets—a cat and a dog—lived happily in a small house in a village by a river.

But Shu did not grow rice. He did not grow anything. In fact, everyone in his village wondered where his rice came from, but that was Shu's secret. No one knew, except—of course—his pets, who were his family.

You see, Shu had once given a travelling monk his last bowl of rice and a place to rest. Even though Shu had hardly any food for himself and his pets, he shared what little he had with the monk, whose cheeks were hollow and very pale.

After the monk had eaten every grain of rice in his bowl, he handed Shu a silver coin. "For your kindness I will give you this magic coin," he said. "Put this coin in a barrel with a few grains of rice, and the barrel will soon be full."

Shu looked at the coin and then into the monk's eyes, sure he was joking. But the monk seemed totally serious. "No matter how much rice you take from the barrel," he promised, "it will always be full."

Shu had tried out the coin as soon as the monk disappeared down the road. Much to his delight, the few grains of rice he placed in his barrel magically filled it to overflowing. Shu and his pets would never go hungry again. Not only that, Shu could sell the rice and use the money to buy other things!

But one day Shu opened his rice barrel and found that it wasn't full. He waited and waited, but it just didn't fill up the way it normally did. Searching the barrel carefully, Shu soon discovered that the magic coin was gone!

Near panic, Shu tried to think of an explanation. Had he been robbed? He wondered. No, it wasn't likely. Maybe the coin had accidentally slipped into the rice he'd sold to someone. Oh, what was he going to do? Without the coin, he wouldn't have any more rice to sell.

Shu's cat and dog hated to see their beloved master in such distress. They did everything they could to cheer him up. The cat gave Shu all the birds she could catch, while her friend the dog tried to take Shu's mind off their troubles with many games of fetch. But nothing worked. Figuring their noses could sniff out the precious coin if they tried hard enough, the cat and dog decided to team up and search the whole village. They searched and searched, smelling every crack and corner until they had scoured the whole town, but didn't have any luck.

"Well," said the dog, tired but still hopeful, "we've looked everywhere on this side of the river, and it's not here. It must be on the other side. Let's look there tomorrow."

Early the next morning, before the sun came up, the two animals set out. Since it was wintertime, the river was frozen and they thought they could easily walk across the ice. But they skidded and slipped, laughing all the way to the other side. They started their search immediately, sniffing everywhere for the coin, and continued day after day, week after week, month after month, refusing to give up. Without the magic coin, they knew their master would go hungry again.

Soon the river began to thaw and the days grew longer. The scent of flowers and growing grass filled the air, sharpening their senses and giving them more energy.

One day, the dog detected a scent that he thought was worth following. "Hey, do you smell that?" he said to the cat.

The cat gracefully swished her tail before sitting down. She raised her nose high up into the wind and inhaled deeply. Yes, she smelled it, too. "Yes! Yes!" she said, her excitement rising. "It's coming from that house!"

The cat and the dog quickly made their way to a big house by the river. Finding one of the doors unlocked, they followed the faint metallic smell of silver into the house. They padded quietly up a grand staircase and crossed a wide hallway that led to a bright room filled with mirrors. In one corner of the room was a wooden chest.

"The trail ends here," said the dog, pressing his nose against the wooden floor urgently. "It's got to be around here somewhere."

The cat had already climbed on top of the chest. "In here," she said. "Come. I can smell it."

The dog tried to lift open the top of the chest. "Uurgh," he said, grunting. "It's locked! Now what are we going to do?"

The cat jumped off the chest, landing next to the dog without making a sound. Calmly, she tiptoed her way around the edges of the room, deep in thought. "We need help," she said after a while.

"Help?" said the dog. "Who can possibly help us?"

"There must be many rats in this old house," she said. "They can chew their way into the chest."

The dog barked several times. It was a good idea. "But why would rats help us," he said, growing exasperated. "They don't like us! We chase them and torture them all the time."

The cat purred and swished her tail. "Well," she said, tipping her head to one side, "we can promise not to bother them for ten years. How about that?"

The dog agreed. He didn't have any better ideas anyway. Before long, they found some rats.

"Fine," said one of them, after hearing the plan. "We'll help you get the coin."

Just as the cat had imagined it, the rats had no trouble gnawing a hole into the chest. In a matter of minutes their search was over, and they had the magic coin back. At long last, the cat and the dog could go home to their master.

Triumphant and bursting with excitement, they stepped out into the sunny yard and made their way over to the river, eager to cross back for home. But they soon realized they had a big problem. The ice had melted, and the weather was so warm that a group of boys were swimming and playing along the water's edge.

"How will we ever cross this river?" cried the cat. "I can't swim!"

"But I can!" said the dog, wagging his tail. "You hold the coin in your mouth and climb on my back. I can carry you across." The cat did as he said, clinging to the dog as he waded into the river. The dog valiantly paddled against the current, barely keeping his head above water.

One of the boys soon caught sight of them. "Look at that!" he said, pointing at the cat and the dog. "I've never seen a boat like that before!"

The other children looked over and began to laugh. But the dog was determined to cross. Panting, he kept his eyes on the opposite bank and stayed on course.

On top, the scared and shivering cat hung on to the dog with all her might. She dug her claws into his back, deeper and deeper.

"Are you okay up there?" the dog asked, knowing how afraid of water his friend was. But before she could answer, the children began laughing hysterically.

"Look at them bobbing up and down!" they said, giggling.

The dog ignored the commotion all around him. His only thought was to bring the coin back to his master. But in spite of her fear, the cat couldn't keep a straight face. She began to think about how silly she must look to the children, all wet and shaking. No matter how hard she tried, the cat couldn't stifle her laughter. When she finally lost control and began to laugh, the silver coin slipped out of her mouth, immediately sinking to the bottom of the river.

"Ack!" she said. "I've dropped the coin!"

As soon as he heard these words, the dog plunged into the rushing waters to save the coin. He was so angry with the cat that he didn't care if she could swim or not. After having searched for the magic coin for months, the foolish cat had lost it!

But no matter how long the dog stayed underwater, no matter how hard he looked, there was no sign of the coin. It had disappeared.

By some miracle, the cat managed to make it to shore, where she shook the water out of her fur and coughed and spat until she'd expelled all the water she'd swallowed. But things would never be the same again between her and the dog.

Once the dog saw the cat, he started to chase her. To escape, the cat did what cats always do: she ran up a tree. She sank her claws into the branch, her fur standing on end. Hissing angrily at the dog, the cat vowed never to trust him again. He had left her to drown!

The dog barked fiercely at her and scratched at the tree trunk, trying to climb up it. He had never been angrier in his entire life.

Both the cat and the dog were ready for a big fight.

But finally, his throat sore from barking, the dog gave up and returned to his master's house. The cat escaped and never returned.

And this is why even today, when more time has passed than you can imagine, cats and dogs don't get along.

But what do you think happened to Shu? He was so happy that at least one of his pets came home he almost forgot about the missing coin. The dog could not forget, though. He couldn't stand to see his master suffer hunger or bear the cold winter. So he sat beside the river each day, trying to figure out a way to get the magic coin back.

One day, the dog saw a fisherman pull a large fish from the water. When the man cut it open, out fell the magic coin. The dog quickly grabbed the coin with his mouth and ran home to his master, who was very pleased to see the coin again. Together they reopened the small rice shop and lived out the rest of their lives very happily.

The Clever Rabbit and Numskull

❧ India ❧

Sulka's whiskers twitched nervously. He tried hard to remember the happy days of long ago. He was once a sprightly young rabbit who spent carefree days bounding about with his friends and rummaging for snacks. But today was to be his last. He was not only going to face a lion, he was going to offer himself up as this terrible lion's meal!

Be brave, he told himself, his chin quivering. *You have had a long life surrounded by other rabbits who loved you. You have been blessed. Remember that you have to do this for the other rabbits—the younger ones who still have their whole lives ahead of them.*

Smiling wistfully, Sulka thought of his wife and twenty-four children. Now they would never be in danger from the lion Numskull. All the animals were afraid of Numskull, and not only because he was fierce. No, lions were fierce by nature. The animals dreaded him because he hunted, chased down, and killed pretty much anything that moved—and very often he would leave his prey out in the hot sun to rot without even eating it.

To put a stop to all this random violence, the animals had decided that a select few would go to Numskull each day and sacrifice themselves for his dinner. This way the old and weak animals could go first, sparing the young and healthy ones. Although many animals would still die, they would at least die with the purpose of feeding another, and their deaths would not be meaningless.

Numskull, of course, thought that this was a great idea. He'd get all the food he could eat and never have to hunt again. "But if you don't show up when you're supposed to," he warned everyone, "I will hunt you all, just as before."

And so today was poor Sulka's day to die. Although he had long ago accepted his fate, it still took all his courage to face Numskull. Every step brought him closer and closer to his death. Every breath was so shallow that he felt as if he were already dying. Numskull would have him for supper! He couldn't imagine a fate worse than this.

A few more paces, and Numskull was towering over him. "You're late!" he roared. "You are also much too small for a meal. There should be at least four of you to satisfy my hunger."

Sulka shrank away from the raging lion, his eyes squeezed shut.

"For this I am going to go back to hunting," said Numskull, "and I am going to start with rabbits!"

The thought of his children being hunted frightened Sulka even more than being torn from limb to limb by this bloodthirsty beast. Then, suddenly, Sulka saw a way out. With Numskull already getting ready to pounce on him, he worked out a plan that he hoped would save his life.

"O great King!" said Sulka, bowing to the lion. "Please forgive me. Please allow me to explain." Sulka did not dare look up, but he felt Numskull's hesitation. "We knew very well that a single rabbit would be too little for a meal for Your Highness, so they sent five of us."

"Five," Numskull repeated. "I see only one. Where are the others?"

"On the way here we met another lion," Sulka said, making up the story as he spoke. "He asked us where we were going, so we told him we were sacrificing our lives to feed you, our great king, Numskull the Lion." Sulka swallowed hard. His throat felt dry, but he went on. "The lion laughed and said, 'Is that so? But I am the king. How can any lion with a silly name like Numskull be the king?'"

Sulka snuck a peek up at Numskull, who was swinging his massive head from side to side, as if very irritated. "The lion let out a big roar," Sulka continued, "and before we could run away he ate the other four rabbits."

Numskull opened his jaws wide and snapped them shut with tremendous force. Sulka could tell he was growing angrier and angrier. Still, Sulka went on: "In fact, he challenged you to a fight and let me live so that I could bring this message to you."

Again, Numskull opened his mouth, this time releasing a blasting roar that seemed to vibrate inside Sulka. "This is the reason I am late, sir," the clever rabbit said, bowing once again. "I hope you understand."

Of course, this was all part of Sulka's plan to fool Numskull. He hadn't seen any other lions, and no other rabbits had been sent with him.

"Where is this thief?" Numskull bellowed. "Take me to him so that I can show him who's king!"

Clever Sulka then led the lion to a deep water well. "Here's the thief's den, Your Highness," he said respectfully. "He lives inside that hole."

Nervously Sulka watched as the dim-witted Numskull peered over the wall and into the well. "Who are you?" thundered the lion, standing on his hind legs. Sulka knew, of course, that Numskull was yelling at his own reflection, but he was almost sure that Numskull was not smart enough to know that.

Not a second later, a lower voice echoed up the well. "Who are you?" it said.

Numskull let out a deep, angry growl, and a deeper, angrier growl came back.

Not realizing that he was hearing his own voice bouncing back at him, Numskull got angrier and roared, "How dare you challenge me!" Again, the voice roared back, even deeper and louder.

Meanwhile, Sulka hid in some bushes, frightened but hopeful that it would all be over soon. It appeared as if his plan was working, and Numskull would finally get what he deserved.

Suddenly, Numskull leaped up onto the well's side, teetering there for a minute before disappearing with a big splash and panicked roar. Relief immediately washed over Sulka. He had tricked Numskull, and now the murderous lion had no escape. He would surely drown!

Soon the story spread throughout the jungle, and animal after animal came to congratulate the clever little rabbit on outwitting the big, mean lion. And for the first time in as long as they could remember, the animals breathed easily, safe from harm at last.

The Crane's Gratitude

❧ Japan ❧

A long time ago, in a little house deep in the
mountains, there lived an old man and an old woman.
They shared a life together that was simple and nothing out of
the ordinary, really, except maybe that it was more quiet than average,
because the couple did not have any children.

One cold winter day, the old man was out collecting wood for the fire
when he heard a strange noise. He looked around until he spotted a large
bird in the distance. He slowly approached the bird, soon realizing that it was a
beautiful crane tangled in some bushes, struggling to free itself.

The closer he came, the more the crane struggled to get away. "Shhh, I'm not
going to hurt you," the old man said gently to the bird. Its long, graceful neck was
twisted at such an angle that the bird could barely even open its beak. The old
man carefully broke away twigs and branches to make room to release it.

28

Once the old man had released the crane and it got back on its feet, it looked for a moment into the man's kind eyes and then flew off into the sky.

That night, as the wind howled and the snow fell, the old couple heard knocking at their door, which was more than a little unusual. Nobody ever came to visit, most especially so late at night and in such bitter weather.

Much to their surprise, shivering outside was a young girl, no more than twelve. "Oh, my!" said the old man. "Come inside. You must be freezing out there."

The girl looked at him with round, moist eyes, and he noticed how gravely beautiful she was, with skin as white as the snow whirling all around her.

Wordlessly, she stepped into the house and sat down by the fire. When her teeth finally stopped chattering, she asked if she could live with them. "I have no family," she said, her voice crisp. "I have no friends. I have nowhere else to go."

The old man and the old woman looked at each other, marveling how anyone so young could have already had such harsh luck in life.

"I can help around the house," she said to them. "And I promise I will work hard."

The old man felt sorry for the girl. "Please stay," he said.

Days quickly turned into weeks, which turned into months and then years. Eventually the couple began to think of the young girl as their daughter.

One particularly tough winter, the old man worried that their money and food supplies were running dangerously low. He decided to tell his wife, but he didn't want the young girl to overhear him. Even though she was now sixteen, the old man wanted her to have a life free from worry.

But the young girl could sense something was wrong, and she quickly discovered the truth. Without hesitating, she decided to help. "I will weave some cloth for you that you can sell in the village."

The old man brightened at the idea. The old woman looked puzzled. How was it that they didn't know their daughter could weave?

"There is just one thing . . ." the girl said to the old couple. "You must not look at me while I am weaving."

The couple thought the girl's request was a little odd, but they promised not to look into the room where she worked.

That very same night, the young girl began to work. She wove all night and well into the next morning. When she came out of the room at long last, she gave the couple a large bundle of the most beautiful cloth they had ever seen.

The old man carried the cloth down into the valley and sold it for a lot of money, which he used to buy enough food for one month.

The time came when the snow should have melted and spring should have arrived, but the snowflakes still fell and the cold winds blew. Eventually, the little family ran out of food again.

As before, the young girl saw that they would starve if she didn't do something. So she went into a room one night to make more cloth, but not before making the old couple promise not to look in on her.

All night and well into the next morning she worked, just as before, the clacking sound of the loom echoing throughout the house.

In the early hours before dawn, the old woman woke up to the sound of the loom and heard a voice crying. She woke the old man, and the two of them went to see if their daughter was all right.

The old man pressed an ear against the door. "But we promised not to look in," he said, hesitating.

"But what is that sound?" the old woman said, frowning. "We can't just pretend we don't hear it!"

The old man put his hand on the door once again, and looked at the old woman uncertainly.

The old woman nodded. "Well, go ahead!"

He pushed the door open a crack and peeked in. Then suddenly he took a step back and gasped.

"What is it?" the old woman said. She pushed him aside and peeked into the room herself. "Oh my!" she cried in surprise.

In the room was a crane plucking out its own feathers, which it was weaving into a beautiful piece of cloth.

The old woman threw open the door, startling the large bird. Then, in the blink of an eye, the bird began to change forms, suddenly becoming the young girl! She now sat before the old couple with her hands folded in her lap, her eyes fixed on them.

The old man stuttered as he tried to explain why they had burst in on her, but the young girl stopped him. "Please," she said, holding up a hand to stop him from speaking. "I understand."

"We are so very sorry," said the old man. "We have not kept our promise to you."

The young girl looked down into her lap. "I am the crane you saved many years ago," she said, "and I came to help you because you were so kind to me. I've made more cloth for you, which will bring you enough money to survive the rest of the winter. But now that you've seen my true form, I can no longer stay with you."

Then the girl stepped out into the fresh morning air, changed back into a crane, and flew off into the changing colors of dawn. The sun's warm glow radiated brilliantly against the snow as the old man and the old woman watched this magical creature, their beloved daughter, fly away from them.

True, they were alone once again, but they would never be lonely. They would always remember and love the young girl who had warmed their hearts.

Why the Tapir Has No Tail

❦ Malaysia ❦

Thin Goat was called "Thin Goat" because no matter how much he ate, he never got any fatter. One night he found out that he was about to be roasted for a small feast.

"We won't be having many people over," Thin Goat heard the farmer saying to his wife. "Thin Goat's around the right size. We can have him for dinner."

Thin Goat was shocked and horrified. All along he thought he'd be the last goat to be slaughtered because he was too thin. He didn't want to die! He had to find a way to escape.

The farmer swung the gates open early the next morning, and all the goats ran out into the field. They were all happy except for Thin Goat. He didn't feel like grazing. He didn't even feel like playing with his friends. One of the other goats noticed he was not himself and asked what was bothering him.

"Last night when you were all sleeping," he explained, "I heard the farmer and his wife talking." Thin Goat took a deep breath before going on. "They want to kill me for tonight's feast."

Hearing that, all the other goats gathered around him and said in horror, "No! You've got to get out of here!" They really liked Thin Goat, for not only was he nice and helpful, he was smart, too.

"But even if I leave this place," reasoned Thin Goat, "what's to stop them from killing any one of you?"

The other goats' eyes widened. "Oh my!" they said. "You're right! We're all in danger."

"We all need to get out of here," said Thin Goat. "But where do we go? If we run into the village, the people will catch us. If we run into the forest, we might be eaten by wild animals."

Since none of the goats knew what to do, Thin Goat had to come up with something.

After all, he was the one in the most danger. It was a good thing he was a quick thinker, and in a matter of seconds came up with a good plan. "Tonight I'll force the gate open," he said, looking at the other goats intently. "We'll all leave quickly and very quietly. No noise at all."

The goats glanced around at one another. "No noise," they repeated, shaking their heads. "We won't make a sound."

At midnight, Thin Goat opened the gate. "Follow me," he whispered. Very quietly, the goats left the pen, one by one. Once they were far from the house, Thin Goat began to run. The other goats did, too. They ran into the thick black night as fast as they could.

The goats journeyed onward until they reached a field of long grass. Nearby was a pond. "Here we have grass to eat and water to drink," said Thin Goat. "Let's make this our home."

The goats planned to live there for a long time, so they set up camp and made it as comfortable as they could. But one day they spotted a leopard stealthily pacing circles around them, which made them very nervous.

"Don't be scared," said Thin Goat, once again thinking on his feet and knowing exactly what to do. "Just listen to me and agree very loudly with what I say."

When Thin Goat was sure the leopard was within hearing distance, he puffed himself up and put on a loud and fierce voice. "There is only one leopard," he announced to the other goats. "There are many more of us." He made sure to speak slowly, carefully pronouncing his words. "We can catch him! It's been a while since we've eaten a scrumptious meal of leopard."

The goats looked at each other uncertainly for a few seconds. Then, finally understanding that Thin Goat was just trying to scare the leopard away, they all answered, "Yes, we can catch him!" Led by Thin Goat, they started to chant in unison, "We will catch him! We will catch him! Ha ha ha!" And their voices echoed into the forest, louder and louder.

The leopard, of course, was quite shaken, even though he had never heard of goats hunting down a leopard. He decided he'd be safer in the forest, and quickly tore off, away from the noisy goats.

Once in the forest, the leopard met a tapir. "Why are you running so fast?" asked the tapir.

The leopard stopped in his tracks, his chest heaving. "There are wild goats in that field," he said, breathless. "They want to catch me."

"That's silly! What kind of goats can catch a leopard?" The tapir laughed, amused by the thought of leopard-eating goats. "I want to see these goats."

"No!" said the leopard, shaking his head vigorously. "It's dangerous. They're very brave goats, and there are many of them."

Again, the tapir laughed. "I don't believe you," he said. "Goats are neither brave nor fierce!"

The leopard was still scared, but since the tapir was laughing, he was beginning to think that maybe he was making a big deal out of nothing. "All right," he said, finally. "I'll take you there, but only if you tie your tail to mine in case you run off and leave me behind." He was afraid to face the goats alone, so he made very sure he tied a strong knot.

The two animals, with their tails tied tightly together, set off to meet the goats.

Along the way, the leopard was still feeling afraid and unsure. "Cheer up! We are going to have great fun," said the tapir, trying to calm him down.

Meanwhile, worried that the leopard would return, Thin Goat climbed on top of a hill to watch out for him. Sure enough, Thin Goat spotted the leopard when he was still very far away. He couldn't be certain, but it looked as if the leopard was now returning with a tapir.

Thin Goat quickly sent the other goats into the forest to eat wild berries, being sure to ask one of them to bring some berries for him to eat, too. As the two figures drew closer, Thin Goat called out to the herd, "Run west *now*!" and all the goats immediately took off stampeding in one direction, their mouths and beards stained and dripping red from having eaten juicy berries.

Thin Goat, his mouth smeared with red, now climbed atop a rock on top of the hill. "Leopard!" he shouted as loudly as he could. "We've just eaten your grandfather. And now we're going to eat you and your friend the tapir!"

Thinking that the goats' mouths were dripping with blood, the tapir was now trembling in terror. "You've tricked me!" he said to the leopard. "I should never have agreed to come with you!" The tapir turned to run away, hoping to escape from these strange, frightening goats.

At that moment, the leopard was too shocked to speak. He, too, wanted to get away as fast as possible. So he turned to run away—but in the other direction!

The leopard felt a pulling, then tugging, then a stretching. Had the goats caught him? Would he be their dinner after all?

"Aaaaahhhhh!" screamed the tapir, as he felt searing hot pain shoot through him.

The leopard turned back to see what had happened, and was horrified. Because his tail had been tied to the tapir's and they had run in opposite directions, he had accidentally torn off the tapir's tail! Now the tapir would have only a stump where his tail had once been.

Baka the Cow and Kalabaw the Water Buffalo

❦ Philippines ❦

Kalabaw the water buffalo raised his nose up to the sky, his rounded horns pointing down toward the cracked soil beneath him. He tipped his head back as far as he could and waited for a breeze. None came. Then he swung his neck around and tried to scratch an itch on his side.

"Aaaak!" he said, turning in circles as he struggled to get at the itch.

He felt like a silly puppy chasing his own tail, and the intense heat from the early morning sun only made him grumpier. Kalabaw never liked the month of May, because it was the hottest, driest time of the year. No matter where he went or what he did, he couldn't seem to get cool.

He was rubbing the itchy spot against a tree when he heard a familiar voice calling. "Kalabaw!" it said. "Kala—BAAAW!"

With a frown Kalabaw peered through a clearing in the bushes and saw his best friend, Baka the cow, trotting over to him. Baka looked as if he had been running. His almost-black hide was frothy with sweat, and his sand-colored legs were darker than usual.

"Oh, it's you!" said Kalabaw, instantly forgetting his itch. He was always happy to see Baka.

"I want to go for a swim," Baka said. "It's so hot! Do you want to come?"

"Yes, of course," Kalabaw said. "Let's go find some thick cool mud to wallow in!"

Laughing and in great excitement, they galloped down a winding path toward the shady river. After jumping over a fallen tree and squeezing between two giant boulders, they arrived at the water's edge. Baka slipped out of his dark, prickly skin as he prepared to jump in. Kalabaw stumbled, still running, as he peeled off his coat. The short hairs of his coat were chocolate-brown around his head and rump, and blond around his belly.

43

They spent the next few hours splashing around, diving for rocks, and swimming from bank to bank to see who was faster. When they finally grew tired, they found a shallow spot right under a talisay tree (sea almond tree) whose branches reached out over the entire width of the river. There they settled, sitting down on their haunches with only their heads poking out above the cool, thick mud.

Kalabaw, the larger of the two, soon began to feel a rumble in his stomach. "I'm so hungry, I could eat a tamaraw (dwarf buffalo)!" he said.

"Well, I think I will!" Baka said, jumping to his feet quite suddenly. He pushed his way through the mud and clambered onto the riverbank. "Last one back to the field is a tamaraw's tail!" he cried, grabbing one of the hides the two friends had hung on a branch for safekeeping.

Kalabaw raised himself out of the sticky mud in one powerful movement and chased after him. With his mouth, he grabbed the other hide and stepped into it as quickly as he could.

In their rush to get dressed, Baka mistakenly put on Kalabaw's skin, and Kalabaw put on Baka's. Neither of them noticed that their skins didn't quite fit until they got back to the field.

"Ha, ha, ha!" Baka laughed. "Look at yourself! You're wearing my coat!"

Kalabaw looked down at his forelegs and was surprised to find that they were now sand-colored. They were supposed to be brown, like chocolate. Puzzled, he quickly checked his back legs, noticing that the skin around his neck felt as if it might tear. They were sand-colored, too! Realizing what had happened, he glanced up at Baka, who was laughing so hard, he was rolling around in the tall grass.

A giggle started to rise up inside Kalabaw as he pointed wordlessly at his friend. "Hee, hee, hee, hee, hee!" was all he could say for a long time. "You look like you lost a hundred kilos in a single morning!"

Baka stopped laughing just long enough to look down at his belly. "Oh no!" he said, looking slightly alarmed. "I can't even see my belly because there's too much skin in the way."

Baka shook his head from side to side, fascinated by the loose skin under his chin, which flapped around with even the slightest movement. As he did so, Kalabaw playfully took a nip at the baggy skin around his neck, which made Baka burst out into a new fit of giggles. "Look!" Baka said, gasping for breath. "I'm an old, old cow!"

Kalabaw took another small nibble and then another and another, and before long they were both rolling around in the grass, laughing.

Soon it was noon. The sun was high up in the sky, hotter than ever, and Kalabaw started to feel uncomfortable in Baka's tight skin, which was now slick

with perspiration. He was also growing more and more hungry, as if he could eat not just a tamaraw but five tamaraws. He stopped laughing, clutching his grumbling stomach as he tried to squeeze himself out of Baka's hide.

"Aaargh! Your skin is too tight and too slippery!" he said as he wriggled around on the ground. "I. Just. Can't. Get. Out. Of. It."

By this time, Baka had also stopped laughing. He was sweaty and covered in dirt and pieces of grass. "Can we go eat now?" he said weakly.

Kalabaw stopped struggling. He let out a long sigh before popping up to his feet. "Fine," he said. "I guess I can get used to your skin. Maybe it will stretch out."

But Baka's skin never did stretch out, and Kalabaw's skin never shrank. They lived the rest of their lives in hides that didn't fit. This is why, to this day, cows' skins seem baggy and too big for them, and water buffaloes' dark hides fit snugly.

How the Sea Became Salty

❦ Japan ❦

Mitsuo and Yasuo were two brothers who never got along, not even when they were little boys. They were just too different. Now that they were grownups, they rarely spoke to one another, although their farmlands lay side by side. Mitsuo owned a big piece of land with plenty of rice, large barns and a beautiful house. Yasuo had a small farm with only a little rice, one barn and a broken-down old house.

One day Yasuo ate the last of his rice. He went next door to ask his brother for something to eat, but Mitsuo snapped at him. "Why should I give you food? You'll just turn around and give it to every lazy beggar that happens to come along."

Mitsuo was greedy and mean, and he never helped people. Yasuo, on the other hand, was generous and kind. He always shared whatever he had, even when he hardly had enough for himself.

Yasuo did not want to fight with his brother, and left peacefully. His stomach gurgled loudly as he wondered what he was going to do. What would he eat? Yasuo considered this problem as he walked, making his way down a winding road that passed his house. Soon he met an old monk who was walking in the other direction.

"What's the matter, my son?" the monk said. "Why do you look so worried?"

"Well, Grandfather," said Yasuo, "today I ate the last of my rice. I am hungry and I don't know what to do." In Japan, it is a sign of respect to call elderly men *grandfather*. Yasuo, always polite, remembered to do this in spite of his hunger.

The old monk smiled. "If you go to the end of this road," he said, "you will see a hillside, and in that hillside a small cave."

Yasuo listened to the monk intently. He did not know what else to do.

"Go inside the cave and see what you find," the old monk said, digging a hand into his pocket. "Take this with you." He handed a *manju*, a small wheat cake, to Yasuo.

Tucking the *manju* into his pocket, Yasuo thanked the monk, headed down the road, and started looking for the cave's opening.

Immediately Yasuo found a tiny hole at the very base of the hill. *Could this be it?* he wondered. He crouched down on his hands and knees and poked his head into the hole. To his astonishment, inside the cave were dozens of miniature people scurrying about. He realized that they were *kobito,* a kind of magical little men and women who live in the woods and hills.

The *kobito* seemed to be busy building something, but when they saw Yasuo they all ran for safety. In the blink of an eye, they had vanished!

Yasuo scratched an eyebrow, wondering what to do next. "Hello!" he said into the mouth of the cave, just above a whisper. "Please don't be afraid. I won't hurt you."

One by one, very slowly, the kobito reappeared. As they eyed him curiously, Yasuo took a closer look at what they were building. It seemed to be a house, but it was not even half finished and would need a lot more work.

"I can help you build your house," he said, looking at one of the *kobito* men. "Would you like me to fetch you more wood?"

The men nodded yes, so Yasuo headed into the forest to gather sticks and twigs. Soon he returned with an armload of wood, which he put near the cave's entrance. He watched as the *kobito* began to build again, moving very quickly and working very hard. Yasuo was sure their labor must have made them hungry, so he offered them his wheat cake. He watched in wonder as the little people gobbled up the *manju* in a matter of seconds.

Despite the hunger deep in his belly, Yasuo grinned broadly. Nothing made him happier than helping others.

Now the *kobito* were laughing and talking loudly. Yasuo stayed out of the way, watching quietly. Finally one of the *kobito* men broke out of the group and approached him. "For bringing us wood and a delicious meal," he said to Yasuo, "we are going to reward you with our greatest treasure."

Yasuo followed the *kobito* to a large rock, which they asked him to move. Under the rock was a hole, and in the hole was a grinding stone made of two flat stones that looked like small wheels. The stones were placed one on top of the other and held together by a wooden peg. There was a hole in the top stone, and next to the hole was a wooden handle.

"If you speak the name of something three times while turning the grinder to the right," the *kobito* man explained, "whatever you name will come out of the hole. To stop things from coming out all you have to do is turn the handle to the right and say 'please stop' and 'thank you.' "

Yasuo picked up the grinder. The stones felt cold and heavy in his hand.

Yasuo felt honored and happy to have received such a magical gift. Holding the grinding stone close to his chest, he thanked the *kobito* and said goodbye.

On his way home, he stopped to eat. He carefully held the grinder and began turning the handle to the left. "*Manju, manju, manju,*" he said as he turned it. True to what the *kobito* had promised and much to his delight, *manju* started popping out of the grinder. Yasuo gathered the cakes until his sack was full and then stuffed his pockets with them. When he had more than enough to eat, he turned the handle to the right to stop the cakes from coming out. "Please stop," Yasuo said to the magic grinder. "Thank you," he added, when no more *manju* appeared.

From that day on Yasuo had everything he wanted. Still, he never forgot how poor he had been, and he continued to help the old, the sick, and the hungry, just as he had before. Soon so many people were coming to Yasuo for help every day that they began to form a long line outside his front door. Sometimes the line snaked all the way out to the road.

It was not long before Mitsuo noticed all the people visiting his brother's humble farm. He also noticed that they arrived empty-handed but left with more food than they could carry. Sometimes they left with clothes. Mitsuo just couldn't understand it. Where was Yasuo, who was so poor, getting everything? Mitsuo knew his brother couldn't possibly afford to buy all those things.

Late one night, Mitsuo decided to sneak over to his brother's house to find out what was going on. He peeked into a window and saw Yasuo bent over the magic grinding stone. "Manju, manju, manju," Yasuo was saying.

So that's it! thought Mitsuo as he watched. *I'll steal that stone and move far, far away. I'll be so rich, I'll never have to work again!*

When Yasuo went to bed, Mitsuo slipped into his house. He filled his pockets with *manju*, grabbed the grinder, and ran out into the night. He ran and ran until he came to the seashore. There he stole a boat and sailed far out into the ocean.

Mitsuo woke up as the sun was rising. Hungry, he ate the *manju* he had brought with him. Now, *manju* are very sweet, so after eating them he wanted something salty to get rid of the sweet taste in his mouth. He took out the magic stone, turned the handle to the left, and said aloud, "Salt, salt, salt."

Well, of course salt came out of the stone right away. Chunks of white salt flew out of the grinding stone in every direction. Mitsuo laughed, happy that the grinder worked so well. Moments later, the bottom of the boat was covered in a thick layer of crunchy salt.

"Okay," Mitsuo said to the stone. "That's enough salt. Stop!"

But the salt kept pouring out. "Stop!"
he said again and again, twisting and pulling the
handle to the right and to the left, his face turning red.
"Stop! I order you to stop!" But nothing happened.

To throw the grinder overboard was unthinkable to the greedy Mitsuo, even though it would have been the smart thing to do.

Faster and faster the salt came, until Mitsuo was buried in salt up to his waist. Only then—having no other options—did he decide to throw the grinder into the ocean. But it was too late, as the boat was already sinking.

Mitsuo drowned, of course, and all the salt spilled into the ocean. The Japanese believe this is how the ocean became salty. To this day, the magic grinding stone continues to produce salt, and it always will.

The Mousedeer Becomes a Judge
❈ Indonesia ❈

Crocodile was resting in his favorite spot under a shady tree. So old was the tree that its roots strained to keep it grounded as it leaned sharply across the river. Suddenly, the wind blew, knocking over the tree with one powerful gust and pinning Crocodile underneath it.

"Help! Help!" cried Crocodile. "I'm stuck! Someone, please help me!"

As the day wore on, Crocodile's cries for help grew weaker and weaker, and still no one came to help him. He was exhausted and very hungry. Soon he didn't even have the energy to thrash his tail around.

Instead, he remained as still as possible, listening intently for a sign of someone who could help him. The sun was beginning to set when he heard heavy thudding footsteps approaching.

"Oh, please!" he said desperately. "Please come and help me!"

Crocodile could now hear the footsteps trotting over to him. He heaved a huge sigh of relief when four hoofed legs stopped and stood squarely before him. He tried to look up to see who it was but couldn't move his head.

"That's a pretty big tree," a deep voice said from above Crocodile.

"Get it off me, please!" Crocodile said, now almost in tears. He recognized the voice as belonging to Buffalo, whom he'd met a couple of times in the past. "I will be forever grateful to you!"

"Relax, Crocodile," said Buffalo in a calm, soothing voice. "Don't worry. I can lift it." Buffalo lowered his head, placed his two horns under the fallen tree, and lifted it off Crocodile's back.

Crocodile scrambled free, swinging his tail around and snapping his jaws open and closed. His back felt as stiff as a board, and he needed very badly to get something to eat.

"Are you all right?" asked the concerned Buffalo.

Crocodile raised his head to look up at Buffalo. He wanted to thank him for saving his life. But when he saw Buffalo's thick neck and fat haunches, he couldn't help imagining how good Buffalo would taste. Instantly his mouth began to water, and a long string of drool dribbled out. He couldn't help it. He wanted a bite out of Buffalo. "Ooooh, my back hurts!" he cried, pretending it hurt more than it actually did. "Buffalo, please carry me deeper into the water."

Careful not to cause Crocodile pain, Buffalo did as he asked. Deeper and deeper they went into the water. Crocodile's stomach was now rumbling loudly, and he could no longer stop himself. With a mean grunt, he took a small nip out of Buffalo's neck.

"Ow!" Buffalo said, howling. "That hurt! What are you trying to do? Eat me?" Buffalo backed away from Crocodile, who had his jaws open once again. "I can't believe it. I just saved your life! You should be showing me a little more gratitude instead of making me your dinner."

Crocodile sneered. "Why should I be grateful?" he said. "Animals need to eat, and right now I'm hungry!"

"But I just helped you, Crocodile," Buffalo replied, shaking his head in disbelief. "Be fair."

"Fair?" Crocodile repeated. "Fair? There has never been fairness or justice in the forest. The strong and the mighty are the ones who decide what's fair."

"Is that so?" said Buffalo. "Well, I believe there's justice in the forest . . . and the unjust will have very bad luck."

Crocodile laughed; as though making fun of Buffalo. "All right," he said. "Let's see about that."

Just then, they spotted the trunk of a banana tree floating down the river. "Ah, let's ask that trunk," said Crocodile.

"Sure," Buffalo agreed. "Hey, Banana Trunk," he called out. "We want to ask you about justice."

The trunk stopped at the edge of the river, and Crocodile explained how he'd been caught under the tree and how Buffalo had set him free. "And now I want to eat Buffalo because I'm hungry," Crocodile said to the trunk, which was rocking back and forth as it listened. "Do you think it's fair if I eat Buffalo?"

The trunk rolled over and wet its other side. For a moment it didn't say anything. "I think it's fair enough," it said after a while. "Justice is like that everywhere. When banana trees are young and bear fruit, people care for us and tend to us," he explained. "But when we become old and worn . . . What do they do? They cut us down and throw us into the river!"

Crocodile nodded. "You see?" he said to Buffalo.

"Yes," said the trunk, resolved. "People say that is justice because *they* hold the power!" And with that the trunk continued its journey down the river.

"As I said," said Crocodile, "the ones who are powerful decide what is just and fair." He lunged once again at Buffalo, his mouth open.

"But that is not fair!" protested Buffalo. "It's certainly not just! Anyway, what does the trunk of a tree know about justice?"

Just then, an old horse approached the river. Buffalo called to him just as he was beginning to drink. "Friend!" he said. "Tell us what is just and what isn't."

"Just?" repeated the horse, looking up.

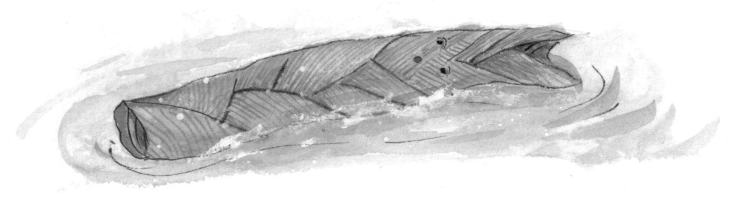

He lifted his head up to the sky and whinnied. "Where is there justice?" he said bitterly. "When I was young and strong, I served my master well. I pulled his cart for many miles every day from the village to the field and then back again to the village. But now that I am old, I am left to fend for myself. There is no justice." Then the horse shook his head and continued on his way.

Crocodile smiled widely and began to open his mouth again.

Buffalo looked about desperately, and spotted his friend Kancil, the mousedeer, prancing through the forest. "Hey, 'Cil!" he yelled. "Come here for a moment."

Kancil approached, and Buffalo asked, "Is it fair or not, 'Cil? The crocodile that I just helped wants to eat me now."

"Patience, patience," said Kancil. "To determine whether something is just or not, I need to understand exactly what happened from the very beginning."

"Yes, that's right," agreed Crocodile.

"So how did it begin?" asked Kancil.

"Well, I was resting under that tree over there when a gust of wind blew it down," explained Crocodile.

"Come," said Kancil. "Let's go to the exact spot."

The three animals approached the fallen tree. "Then what happened?" asked Kancil. "Well, 'Cil," said Crocodile. "I was lying here and the tree fell on top of me."

Kancil waved to Buffalo. "Here, brother Buffalo, lift this tree so that it rests on Crocodile again."

Buffalo slipped his horns under the tree, lifted it up, and shifted it to rest on Crocodile's back. "It was like this," he explained.

"Ah! It hurts!" said Crocodile, moaning. "Get it off me!"

"But was it indeed like this?" asked Kancil.

Crocodile yelped in pain. "Yes! But, oh, oh, it hurts!"

"Oh, so it was just like this," stated Kancil as Crocodile struggled under the weight of the tree. "Well, I see—"

"Please!" said Crocodile. "Get it off me!"

"But isn't this justice?" Kancil went on. "If the tree fell on you, then let the tree lie on you," he reasoned, "because when you were helped, you repaid the act of kindness by threatening the one who helped you."

Crocodile was seeing stars, the pain was so intense. He could barely understand what Kancil was saying, but he knew he didn't like it at all.

"Come on, Buffalo," Kancil said in cheery voice. "Let's go."

Kancil and Buffalo then strolled off together, leaving Crocodile to suffer his just reward.

The Fake Gem
❦ Thailand ❦

Phra pinched the green stone between his thumb and forefinger, and held it up against the sunshine pouring in through the window. It glistened and made little specks of light bounce off the cracked walls of his shop in downtown Bangkok. The stone certainly sparkled like a precious gem, perhaps an emerald, but Phra knew it was nothing more than a piece of glass. He had been trading gems for so long, he could tell just by looking at it.

He cupped the stone in his palm and chuckled. "This is a joke, right, Nai?"

Nai was an old friend who had recently had a run of bad luck with money. He had come into Phra's shop to sell some jewelry for cash. "No, it's not a joke," said Nai in a serious tone. "That stone has been in my family for generations, and it's worth a lot."

"Nai!" Phra said, smiling at his friend. "This is a piece of glass!"

"Please, Phra," said Nai. "Take a closer look. It is a very unusual gem. I would rather not sell it at all, but my family has become very poor, and we need to eat."

"But, Nai—" Phra began again.

"Please!" Nai said, interrupting. "Please help me sell it."

Phra hesitated. How could he possibly sell the stone as something precious when he knew very well it is not? He didn't want to lie to people. All his life he had been honest and hard-working, and that's why he was successful. Everyone knew they could trust him. The king of Thailand came to buy jewels from him, and even princes from faraway countries journeyed to Bangkok to visit his humble shop.

"Listen to me," said Nai. "You just think it's glass because it's so rare. It does not look like any gem you've ever seen before." He looked straight into Phra's eyes. "You have to believe me."

Nai didn't seem to be joking. He didn't seem to want to leave the shop, either, though it was getting very late. He'd been there for hours, repeating his pleas over and over again. Finally, just before closing time, Phra reluctantly took the piece of glass from Nai and shoved it into a drawer. He still wasn't convinced, but he took the stone just to make Nai go away.

A few weeks later, a Chinese man came into Phra's shop. He introduced himself as Lao and explained that he had been sent to buy gems for a crown being made for the emperor of China. "I hear you are the most important and honest jeweler in Bangkok, and that you have the best service," Lao said, "so I am visiting you before going to any other shops."

Phra was flattered and felt very proud indeed! He served his special Thai tea and delicious cakes made from fresh coconut. Then he brought out his best emeralds, rubies, and diamonds for Lao to see. He was sure he had the highest quality gems. But as the hours went by, Phra was no longer so certain. None of his gems seemed to impress Lao, who held up each stone against the morning light, shaking his head before putting it down again.

From morning till night, Phra brought out more and more of his gems. Lao meticulously examined each, but all the while he had a frown on his face. Nothing pleased him, not even Phra's special collection of sapphires.

"Too many flaws."

"Not bright enough."

"Too small," Lao said. "I don't want any of them. Perhaps you are not the best jeweler after all."

Not the best jeweler? Phra felt terribly insulted. How dare this stranger criticize him! *Lao would not find better gems anywhere in the world,* Phra thought. He was also annoyed that Lao had taken up so much of his time. In fact, he wished he would just go away.

"Is that all you have to show me?" Lao said. "Is this everything you have?" Phra clenched his teeth together to stop himself from saying something mean. He was getting very annoyed.

As Phra was putting away his large collection of sapphires, he suddenly remembered the piece of glass that Nai had given him. If he showed it to Lao and Lao liked it, it would prove once and for all that Lao knew absolutely nothing about gems.

He slowly slid open the drawer and brought out the piece of glass. "Here's something you might like," he said, gently setting it down in front of Lao.

"Oh!" exclaimed Lao as soon as he saw it. "It's stunning!"

Phra fixed a smile on his face, secretly pleased. He was right. Lao didn't know the first thing about stones. He wouldn't know a good jeweler if he gave birth to one!

Lao was now holding up the piece of glass and squinting as if to take a closer look. "I'll take it," he said, now smiling. "How much do you want?"

"How much?" Lao said again, looking at Phra.

Phra didn't say anything. He had been honest his whole life, and lying did not come easily to him.

Lao clutched the green glass tight in his hand. "I'll give you twenty-five chang for it."

Wow, twenty-five chang is a lot of money! thought Phra. He opened his mouth to speak, but didn't know what to say. He hadn't thought Lao would make an actual offer for the stone and now he wasn't sure what to do. Phra remained silent.

"Fine," Lao said, putting a hand in his pocket and shaking his head. He sighed heavily. "I'll give you thirty chang. But I have only five chang with me. I will leave it with you. Hold the gem for me and I will be back next week with the rest of the money." Lao took out five chang and placed it on the counter.

Feeling guilty, Phra started to confess. "But the gem—" he began.

Before Phra could say another word, Lao interrupted, "No buts! You must sell this gem to me. I insist, and will return for it soon." Lao hurried from the store, leaving his money behind.

Phra just wanted to close shop and go home. It had been a long day and he was tired and hungry. If Lao insisted he wanted to buy the stone, then so be it.

But while walking home through the quiet of the nighttime city, Phra suddenly felt the weight of what he had just done. It wasn't right to cheat anyone, even someone as irritating, insulting, and ignorant as Lao. The shame he felt for the way he'd acted was more than Phra could bear. *How will I ever get out of this mess?* he worried. Phra walked for block after block, deep in thought, and finally reached a decision. *I will face Lao and tell him I can't sell him the gem. I will give him back his money,* he vowed.

Suddenly, a voice called out from behind him. "Phra! Phra!"

Phra turned and looked up the street. It was Nai. He looked as if he was in a big rush.

"A man from China has come to town today," Nai said, catching his breath. "He's looking for gems to buy, so I have come to take back my gem to sell to him."

Phra found himself in a tight spot. The "man from China" was obviously Lao. He felt bad and said, "You know what? I've decided that I want your stone. I'll give you ten chang for it."

Nai paused to think. "Ten chang is not very much for a stone that big," he said after a moment, "but since you're a friend, I'll let you have it." So Phra bought Nai's worthless piece of glass for ten chang.

The thought of Lao's thirty chang still tempted him, but he had made up his mind. His good reputation was worth more than money. All Phra wanted to do was tell Lao that the stone was a piece of glass and return his five chang. After that, he could forget all about the whole thing. But a week went by and Lao never came back. Then two weeks passed and still there was no sign of Lao.

On the third week Phra began to suspect that Nai had tricked him. By the fourth week, Phra was certain he'd been fooled. Lao wasn't from China. Nai had sent Lao to trick Phra, and now Phra had been cheated out of money. Oh, how foolish he had been! He had merely thought about acting dishonestly, and *he* was the one who was cheated.

From then on, Phra was always honest and careful in whatever he did, and even whatever he thought. In doing so, he remained the most important and honest jeweler in Thailand.

The Golden Ring

❧ Philippines ❧

Ganador was the champion cockfighting rooster of Zamboanga province in the South of the Philippines. In the days he was still fighting, none of the other roosters could beat him. He was not only fast and brave, but intelligent, too. Because of his fame, all the other chickens—hens and roosters alike—paid him great respect and he ruled over the best brood pen on the farm. He lived with the farm's most prized hen, his wife, Inahin, as well as all her sisters and female cousins and their many chicks.

Ganador's reputation as the most fearless of fighting roosters even earned him the friendship of Lawin, a powerful giant hawk, who normally looked down on chickens. Although Lawin spent most of his days soaring through the air, preying on snakes and other small animals, he would fly in from time to time to visit Ganador.

The two birds very much enjoyed one another's company, and would perch side by side on Ganador's tepee, usually soon after Lawin's noontime meal.

One such afternoon, as Lawin stretched out his talons midflight, ready to land on the tepee next to his friend, an unmistakable golden glint caught Ganador's eye, blinding him. It was coming from one of Lawin's front toes.

"Bok, bok, bo-ok!" Ganador squawked as he buried his head under his wing to protect his eyes. "What on earth is that?"

"You're awfully timid for a former fighter," Lawin replied, apparently amused. "It's a ring. I found it this morning." He held out his toe and patiently stood on one leg so that Ganador could have a better look.

Ganador peered out from under his wing. The ring gleamed in the sunlight. "Oh, wow!" he said, now noticing the delicate design etched around the ring. "My wife would go crazy if she saw that piece of jewelry."

"It is beautiful." Lawin twisted the ring around his toe with his hooked beak. "I spotted it in the bushes from way, way up high!" he boasted.

Ganador admired the ring for another moment. He wondered if Lawin would consider lending it to him for a day. He wanted to show it to Inahin. "Um . . . Do you—" he said, hesitating.

Lawin lowered his talon. He cocked his head as if to listen more closely to what Ganador had to say. "Yes?"

"Do you— Do you think I could maybe borrow it?"

Lawin twirled the ring around one more time and looked at his friend intently. The feathers around Ganador's neck fluffed up every time Lawin looked at him in that piercing way, each of his eyes a big, black shiny spot evenly encircled by white. He wouldn't admit it to anyone, but he would never want to fight Lawin.

Slipping it off with his beak, Lawin held out the ring and Ganador took it. "Yes, of course," Lawin said, watching as Ganador carefully placed the ring on his toe. "I trust you."

"Oh, thank you!" Ganador said, nodding his head up and down several times. "I promise to return it the next time you drop in."

"Well, then, I'm off," said Lawin, flapping his broad wings and pushing off from the perch. "See you tomorrow!"

Ganador crowed a long good-bye. He watched the hawk's silhouette grow smaller and smaller as Lawin flew high up into the clear blue sky. A second later he was just a tiny speck, and then he disappeared altogether.

Ganador hopped off his perch and rushed over to the brood pen, half-running and half-flying. He was terribly excited to show the ring to Inahin. As he expected, she fell in love with the ring as soon as she laid eyes on it.

"But it's not ours to keep," Ganador was sure to explain to her. "It belongs to Lawin."

The sight of the ring on her toe thrilled Inahin, and she clucked in pleasure as she raised her leg up to admire it. "Oh, it's so beautiful and heavy! I'm going out right now to show everyone!" She rushed off after giving Ganador a peck on the cheek.

Ganador chuckled, delighted that he had made his pretty wife so happy. "Bok, bok, bo-ok!" he cried out after her.

But only minutes after Inahin had left her nest, Ganador heard her cry out in distress. Dust flying everywhere, he flew out of the shed in a panic to find out what happened. He soon discovered that Inahin had dropped the ring on the ground and was now frantically scratching the soil in search of it.

"Bak, bak, bak, bak!" she was saying in a high-pitched, panicked voice. "But I dropped it right here! How can it be lost?"

Ganador swallowed nervously. He could tell by the way her tail was wiggling that she was upset. Hardly anything upset Inahin.

"Calm down," he told her, even though he, too, was anything but calm. "We'll find it. We will."

Pretty soon all Inahin's sisters and cousins had joined the mission to find the ring. With eyes cast downward and heads bowed, all the chickens carefully sifted through the dirt in the pen. Even after the sun went down, they continued to look.

When the sun rose the next day and they still hadn't found the ring, Ganador began to wonder if Lawin would challenge him to a fight once he learned it was missing. The thought filled him with dread. He had retired from fighting long ago, and he was in no shape to be taking on a hawk! Still, he knew it was his duty to protect his roost, and he would have to fight if challenged.

In the early afternoon Lawin returned. He was very upset when Ganador told him the ring was lost. "I don't believe you. You are hiding it," Lawin said angrily.

"Now, wait just a minute," Ganador said, puffing out his chest and raising the feathers around his neck defensively.

"If you don't return it," Lawin said, straightening to his full height. "I am going to eat your chicks one by one until they're all gone!"

Ganador felt the ground hard beneath him and dug his claws into it nervously. "You got to believe me, Lawin," he said, begging. "It was an accident. We dropped the ring. You can see for yourself that we're looking for it."

Without warning, Lawin spread his wings and rocketed into the sky before
Ganador could stop him. The great hawk circled menacingly before swiftly
swooping down, and—despite Ganador's best effort to block him—plucking one of
the baby chicks right off the ground with his giant talons. Off he flew, clutching
the chick.

Ganador and Inahin never recovered from the heartbreak caused by the lost
ring, and they told their story again and again. Soon it was legend in the
barnyard. To this day when we see roosters, hens, and even baby chickens
scratching at the ground with their heads bowed down, they are searching for
Lawin's ring. They have never stopped trying to find it because every now and
then Lawin swoops down and steals another chick.

Liang and His Magic Brush

❧ China ❧

Long, long ago in faraway China, there lived a poor boy named Liang. Both of his parents had died, and he had to take care of himself. To make his living, Liang sold firewood, but he carried in his heart a dream of becoming a great painter. This was all he could think about. Each night he would dream of painting mountains, birds, people, and animals. But Liang was so poor, he couldn't even afford to buy a brush to paint with.

One day, as he was walking along a street in his village, Liang passed a school where a teacher was showing his students how to paint. Liang was fascinated. He stood on tiptoe and peered into a window for as long as he could, just watching how the teacher applied paint to his paper scroll, stroke by stroke. To get a better look, Liang slipped quietly into the school.

When the teacher finished, Liang walked up to him and bowed very low. "Please, sir," he said as politely as he could, "I also want to learn how to paint. Would you please lend me a brush?"

The teacher's face hardened, and he looked as if he were smelling rotten eggs. "Who let this beggar in here?" he said, raising his voice. "Throw him out!"

The students in the painting class chased Liang out of the school, teasing and laughing at him.

But Liang didn't give up on his dream. He decided to practice every day, even if he couldn't afford a brush.

When he went up into the mountains to gather firewood, he would use a twig to draw birds and animals in the dirt. When he went to the river to fish, he would draw in the sand.

He practiced every chance he had and soon became very good. His drawings looked so real that people who saw them expected them to come to life. But Liang still didn't have a brush.

One night a kind-looking old man awoke Liang and handed him something. Liang instantly knew that he shouldn't fear this stranger, and accepted his gift. "This is a magic brush," the old man said. "But always be very careful how you use it."

Liang looked at it carefully. It was a fine brush made of rabbit hair and red sandalwood. Liang looked up to thank the old man, but he was already gone. Liang was so excited that he couldn't get back to sleep.

He got up and began to paint a bird. As soon as he was finished, the bird came to life and flew away. He painted a fish, and sure enough, as soon as it was completed, it came to life. Liang was as happy as he could be. He carefully picked up the fish and carried it down to the stream. The happy fish swam away with a splash.

Every day after that, Liang would paint with his magic brush for the poor people in his village. He would paint hoes, plows, oil lamps, and anything else the villagers needed.

The people of Liang's village were all tenant farmers. That means they farmed the land of a rich landlord. They kept part of what they grew for themselves, but they had to give most of the harvest to the landlord as rent. Liang's landlord was an especially nasty man who went out of his way to make the villagers suffer.

Well, once word of Liang's magic brush got out, the rich landlord heard about it too. The landlord sent out some men to grab Liang and drag him back to his house.

But Liang refused to paint anything for the awful old landlord, no matter what he said. So the landlord threw Liang into a cold, dark, empty barn and left him there to starve.

Late that night it began to snow. It was very, very cold outside. Still, the mean landlord left Liang in the barn with nothing to eat and no way to stay warm. Liang thought about how to escape, but he was hungry and cold, so he decided to do something about that first.

When the landlord finally returned to the barn three days later, he found Liang happily eating hot rice cakes. Not only that, Liang had painted a stove, a steaming pot of hot stew, and a nice thick mattress with his magic brush.

The landlord was so mad that he sent his biggest, roughest men into the barn to force Liang to paint for him. Before anyone could catch him, though, Liang painted a door on the back wall of the barn and ran outside.

All the men ran out after him, but he quickly painted a horse and rode away.

Liang galloped on and on. Over mountains and hills, through valleys, and across plains he raced. At last he came to a town that was quite a distance from his village, and he decided to stay there. He began to sell pictures in the marketplace, but to keep them from becoming real, he didn't finish them. He would paint a bird without one leg or an animal without an eye or an ear.

One day, when Liang had just finished painting a bird without eyes, he accidentally splashed some paint where they should have been. The bird opened its eyes and flew away. All of the townspeople were amazed. Word of Liang's magic brush spread like wildfire, travelling even farther and faster than it had in his own village. Soon even the emperor heard about it and sent out his guards to find Liang and bring him to the palace. Liang had heard many stories about how mean the emperor was to poor people, but he was not afraid.

At the palace, when the emperor told Liang to paint a dragon, he painted a toad instead. When the emperor told him to paint a crane, he painted a chicken. Well, emperors usually get rather upset when people don't do what they say, and this emperor was no exception. He got so angry that he had Liang thrown into jail, and he took away his magic brush.

Eager to increase his huge fortune, the emperor then tried to use the magic brush himself to paint some gold coins, but the coins turned into rocks. When he tried to paint gold bars, they turned into snakes.

The emperor realized that only Liang could use the brush properly, so he let the boy out of jail and gave him a great deal of money. He also gave Liang presents and tried to win his friendship. Liang pretended to go along with this, but no matter what the emperor said or how many presents he gave Liang, the boy somehow remembered the kind of person the emperor really was in his heart.

The emperor, determined to get Liang to paint for him, decided to take him out of the palace one day. "What a great day to spend by the seaside!" he said. "The fresh air will be good for everyone. We shall have so much fun." And off they went—the emperor, the courtiers, and Liang.

On the way, the emperor told Liang how he had always wished to sail to other lands across the ocean.

When they arrived by the seaside, the emperor asked Liang in the sweetest and most polite way possible, "Would you please be so kind and paint me a boat?" So Liang painted a magnificent dragon boat that was fit for an emperor. The emperor, of course, was delighted. His plan was working.

"Now I can go sailing," the emperor said, his eyes shining, "but I will need to bring along some gifts for the people I visit across the ocean." He flashed Liang his sweetest smile. "Please paint me some cloth, food, and provisions for the journey. Oh, and some chests filled with gold coins would be nice too."

So Liang painted bales of fine silk cloth, jars and urns of food and provisions, and chests filled with gold coins.

When the greedy emperor saw the gold, he got quite excited.

"More!" he said, trying very hard to keep his composure. "Paint more gold!" So Liang painted ten more chests of gold coins.

But still it was not enough, and soon the emperor was shouting, "An emperor like me will need more than this to travel. I need gold bars—lots of gold bars!" So Liang continued to paint.

"More! More! More gold!" screamed the emperor, turning red, as he was boarding the boat with his courtiers. "Fill the boat up with gold!"

Liang kept painting more and more gold. Soon the dragon boat was overloaded with gold coins and gold bars.

"Now paint me a good strong wind!" the emperor ordered.

Liang obediently painted the wind, and the heavily laden boat set sail quickly. Not long afterwards, however, it started to sink. The boat was much too heavy to be seaworthy and it sank to the bottom of the ocean, never to be seen again.

The story of Liang and his magic brush spread throughout the country, but no one knew what happened to little Liang. Some said he went back to his village and lived with his friends. Others claimed that he spent his life wandering the earth, painting for poor people wherever he went.

A Tale of Sticks and Turnips
❧ KOREA ❧

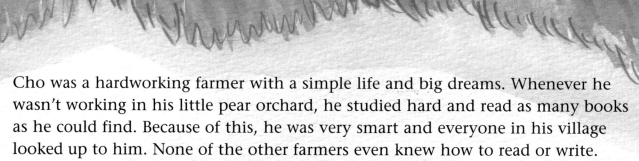

Cho was a hardworking farmer with a simple life and big dreams. Whenever he wasn't working in his little pear orchard, he studied hard and read as many books as he could find. Because of this, he was very smart and everyone in his village looked up to him. None of the other farmers even knew how to read or write.

One day, Cho and his best friend, Shin, were drinking tea and watching the sun set while discussing how to better grow their special pears. "We should take turns bringing our village's crops to the city to sell, so no one man has to leave his farm many times during the growing season," Cho said thoughtfully.

"I agree," Shin replied. "And you're just the person to talk to the villagers about it. Everyone will listen to you—you're practically our mayor. In fact," he continued, "you should be made the official mayor of this village. No one else could ever look after the people who live here as well as you do."

"You know very well that nobody can be mayor, or even get a job in a government office, without passing the royal exam, which is very difficult. And anyway, no matter how many times I write to the governor to apply for the exam, I still hear nothing back." Cho sighed. "It is because I am only a simple farmer."

Shin seemed to be thinking. "Well," he said after a moment, "maybe you should go to the governor's office in the city and speak with him in person."

Cho realized that doing this might be his only chance to sit for the royal exam. If he wanted to be able to help the people of his village, he would have to try again and again until he succeeded.

"You're right, Shin," Cho finally said. "Tomorrow I will travel to the city, and I will not leave until I see the governor himself."

Cho started his trip long before sunrise the next day, bringing with him only some food and water for the journey and a small basket of pears from his most prized tree. When visiting others, the people of Cho's village always brought a gift. Cho planned give these pears, the result of all his hard work, to the governor.

After traveling eight long hours by foot, Cho finally arrived at the big city gates. As he walked through the crowded marketplace, carefully guarding his small basket of pears, his excitement almost made him forget how tired he felt. When he reached the governor's office, two men were guarding the door. "Please," Cho said, not even sure if the men were listening. "I have no appointment, but I wish to see the governor."

"The governor is a very busy man, so you can keep wishing," replied one of the guards. "Maybe you'll see him next spring, if you're lucky." The guard laughed and turned away.

But Cho would not give up so easily. He decided to wait, hoping to meet the governor as he left for the day.

Many hours later, a man in royal garb was escorted past the guards. Cho quickly kneeled in the path of these new men, saying in a loud voice, "Mister Governor, please spare me a few minutes of your time! I am farmer Cho, and I have come to ask permission to sit for the royal exam. I've been studying for many years. Please give me a chance." Seeing that the governor was ready to step around him, Cho quickly continued, "I've brought a small gift of fruit from my village." He handed the basket to one of the guards.

The governor eyed the delicious-looking pears. "Go home," he told Cho. "You will hear from me when you can come sit for the exam."

So Cho went home, where he waited patiently until a year had passed. Still he heard nothing from the governor. He was disappointed, but with encouragement from Shin and his wife, Cho decided to return to the city to see the governor.

But halfway through Cho's journey, the sky suddenly darkened and the wind picked up. Seconds later, rain started to come down hard. Cho realized he needed shelter from this storm. Up ahead, a strange hut appeared out of nowhere, and he struggled towards it. The hut's door flew open just as Cho raised his hand to knock on it, startling him. Inside, the hut was more comfortable than Cho had expected. The friendly young couple who lived there offered him plenty to eat and drink.

Cho was drifting off to sleep at the dinner table when he felt a tapping sensation all over his body. It was strange, almost as if someone were lightly beating sticks against his skin. But Cho was far too sleepy to do anything about it.

He woke up to a terrible headache and the sound of murmuring voices. One of the voices was saying, "It's time to take the ox to the market." Cho opened his eyes slowly. As he did, he noticed something very different about himself. Right before his eyes, which were now widening in horror, was an animal's gray snout. Not only that, it was attached to his face, where his nose was supposed to be!

Confused and very afraid, Cho struggled to stand up. As he did, he clumsily

fell to the floor with a loud thud. Cho felt a scream rising in his throat, but no sound came out. His hands and feet had turned into hard clattering hooves, and for some reason the only sounds he could make were throaty grunts.

"Whoa!" said the woman he'd had dinner with the night before. "Hold steady." *Hold steady? Why is she talking to me this way?* wondered Cho. Then it suddenly dawned on him. Snout, hooves, grunting sounds … why, Cho had somehow turned into an ox!

Cho was too stunned to move. He couldn't even fight back when the woman put a ring through his nose and tied him to the end of a rope.

The man took the rope from his wife and began to lead Cho to the market. On the way, the man carefully tied Cho to a stake near an inn and went inside.

Cho had to act quickly. He didn't want to end up hanging in a butcher's shop.

Using all his strength, he pulled the stake right out of the ground and fled. He ran and ran on his strange four legs, and before long came to a turnip patch. The turnips looked succulent and juicy, so Cho ate a few of them. To his great surprise, he turned back into a man!

"Aaaahh," said Cho, exhaling with great relief. He ran all the way home.

Cho slept for three whole days after he arrived back at his farm. When he woke up, he remembered what had happened, although now it seemed like a bad dream.

He decided it would be best if he said nothing about it—not even to his wife.

As the months flew by, he thought less and less about that bizarre night the strange couple had turned him into an ox. But one day he heard from his wife about the governor's latest misfortune.

"Can you imagine?" she said. "The governor's son has turned into an ox! Everyone is saying that an evil curse has been put on him."

Cho only nodded. "I'm going to the market," he said, pretending not to be especially interested in the gossip.

Immediately he set out for the market and bought some turnips. He dried them in an oven and ground them into a powder. Carrying the powder in a small sack, Cho travelled to the governor's house. There he found a crush of people hoping to catch a glimpse of the boy-turned-ox.

"Stand back!" he said, pushing through the crowd. "Let me pass!"

Cho finally arrived at the gates leading to the governor's home and approached one of the guards. "I am here to help the governor's son," he said. "Please. The child needs me. I'm his only chance. I can break the curse."

A servant soon arrived to lead Cho to the boy, who had indeed turned into an

ox and was now swatting a fly with his tail. Six doctors were huddled together, deep in discussion. The governor was slumped in a chair nearby.

Cho cleared his throat to speak. "I think I can help you," he said.

The governor got up from his chair and put an arm around the ox. "He is my only son," he said desperately. "Do you really think you can help him?"

"Yes," said Cho, feeling very sure that he could.

Showing no sign at all of recognizing Cho, the governor moved aside to make way for him. "Please help my son," he pleaded.

Cho stepped up to the ox and presented it with a handful of turnip powder. "Go on," whispered Cho gently. "Eat it."

The ox sniffed at the chalky powder before dipping his tongue into it. The very next instant the beast turned into a wide-eyed little boy sitting on the floor.

The governor threw his hands up to the sky. "Oh! It's a miracle," he said, his eyes brimming with tears. Taking Cho's hand in both of his, he said, "Thank you, thank you. For this I will give you any reward you want."

"I would like to take the royal exam," Cho eagerly replied.

"Then you will," the governor answered with a smile. "You are a good man. You will do well serving the government."

A week later, Cho passed the exam and the job he had been wanting for so long became his. His dream of helping others finally came true. As mayor, he was able to do many good things for the people and his village prospered.

The Lucky Farmer Becomes King
❧ Thailand ❧

"Someday I will be king," Lek said to his wife, Ying.

Ying only smiled. "My dear husband," she said, as she always did, "you are a rice farmer with a tiny piece of land. I love you very much, but maybe you should put away your daydreaming and get back to work."

"Oh, you'll see," Lek told his wife. "One day you will eat those words." With that, he got back to work, dreaming of the day he'd mount the royal elephant and live in the royal palace. Deep in his heart he knew that day would come. He didn't care if his wife thought he was only a silly man with big dreams.

One day, while Lek and Ying were planting rice under the hot sun, Ying suddenly cried out, "What was that?" She stood upright, turning around to look behind her. "Listen, Lek!"

Standing knee-deep in the rice paddy, Lek listened but couldn't hear a thing.

"Shhh!" Ying said, quickly picking up a whittling knife that was nearby. "It's a growling sound. Can't you hear it?"

Again, Lek listened. He was about to sidle up next to Ying, when she suddenly screamed. Lek looked in the direction she was facing and saw an enormous bear rushing toward them. "Run!" he shouted. "Run!"

Without turning back, Lek ran for his life. He stormed into his house, slammed the door shut, and barred it behind him. He was so afraid that he didn't realize that he'd locked Ying out, too. Trembling, he peeked through a crack in the door and saw that the beast was less than two meters away from his wife, ready to attack her. Lek was frozen with fear.

In Ying's upraised hand was his whittling knife. Lek closed his eyes just as the bear roared, flashing its long white teeth and raising its giant paws. It was too late to do anything to save poor Ying.

Suddenly Lek collapsed and huddled into a ball, crying. He was sure his wife had just been killed by a wild animal. Nothing could be worse! Several minutes passed, and then he heard a voice. "Open the door," it said. "Please."

Lek couldn't believe it. It sounded like Ying.

"Open up, Lek. The bear is dead," Ying said weakly.

Lek got up and very carefully peered through the crack in the door. The second he saw his wife, the color returned to his face. "Oh, you're alive!" he cried, as he flung the door wide open. "I'm so sorry. My legs just wouldn't move," said Lek, wrapping his arms around Ying and sobbing.

Ying was too shaken to say anything. Fortunately, she was not hurt. When she had found the door was locked, she had no choice but to turn around and face the charging bear. Luckily, it charged right into the whittling knife she had held clutched in both hands.

Lek finally stopped crying and began to feel like himself again. He started to realize that if people heard his wife had killed the bear, while he'd locked himself in the house, they would think he was a coward. "What will you say if someone asks who killed the bear?" he asked Ying.

Ying shot him a quizzical look. "I'll tell the truth," she said. "What kind of question is that?"

"Well," said Lek, stammering a bit, "people might, uh, misunderstand if you tell them the truth." He looked at his wife and measured his words carefully. "Not very many women have killed bears, you know. Some people might be afraid of you . . . and some might even believe you killed the bear with black magic."

Ying merely shrugged in response.

"My dear," Lek went on, "to protect you from what people might say about you, why don't we say that I killed the bear?"

"Fine," said Ying. "It really makes no difference to me."

Before long, news of the bear-slaying reached the palace and Lek was summoned by the king, who had always honored bear-killers.

"Well done, my good man. You shall be rewarded." Then the king gave Lek six rubies, two emeralds, and one sapphire. But, most importantly, he gave Lek a new title. He bestowed upon him the glorious name Hon Mee, which meant Brave Bear-Killer. Lek was no longer just a simple rice farmer. Before long, everyone in the country would speak of him as the best bear-hunter in all the land.

The king even invited Lek to live at the palace, and for the first time in his life Lek was truly happy. He loved the leisurely life of the palace and delighted in the luxury of royal treatment. The soft silks felt wonderful against his skin, especially in comparison to the rough cottons he used to wear. The savory curries and sweet meats were far more delicious to Lek than rice and fish. All day and every day, he smiled.

He returned home to see Ying and told her that he would one day be king. Only then would he take her to the palace. Happy to see Lek, she just hugged him.

Lek's happiness did not last long. A giant cobra named Chong Ra-Ang soon slithered onto the palace grounds, causing trouble for those who lived there. When the king heard about the snake, which holed itself up in the palace well, he summoned Lek.

102

"Brave Bear-Killer," he said, "you must remove the cobra from our well."

Lek was terrified, of course. He did not want to face Chong Ra-Ang, but the king had given him a direct order. Lek crept backward on his hands and knees, shaking and perspiring from nervousness, until he was out of the king's sight.

Having no choice, Lek went to the well to see what he could do. "I am strong and brave!" he said to himself, over and over.

He peered over the side of the well to get a better look at the creature, but in doing so he tripped over a stone and lost his balance. Lek fell, tumbling straight into the well, landing right on top of Chong Ra-Ang!

Lek did not know how to swim and was now flailing his arms around, trying to keep his head above water. He swung wildly and reached out for something, anything to help him stay afloat. He grabbed the snake just as it was raising its enormous head to strike, and jumped on its back. Lek squeezed Chong Ra-Ang so tightly that the snake was killed instantly. No one was more surprised than Lek when he realized what had happened.

"Help! Help!" he called out as loudly as he could. By now he was really going under.

Luckily, someone heard him and quickly lowered ropes to pull him and the dead snake out of the well.

The king smiled happily when Lek showed him the dead cobra. "Hon Mee, good job!" said the king, "You have earned another reward." He gave Lek twelve rubies, six sapphires, and two glittering white diamonds. Better than anything else, however, was the gift of a new title, Hon Mee Chong Ra-Ang, which meant Brave Bear- and Snake-Killer.

Again, Lek settled down to a comfortable life in the palace. The servants pampered him. He grew plump and lazy, but never forgot his dream of being king.

The next time he visited Ying, he told her how he had killed the snake with his bare hands and told her again that soon she would be living in the palace. That night, Lek talked and talked until the crow of the rooster reminded him that it was time to return to the palace.

On the way back, a group of little children came out to cheer him. Villagers gathered around him, begging for stories of his brave deeds. He declined modestly, and in doing so became even more famous. People from all over adored Lek, now known as Hon Mee Chong Ra-Ang, and cheered at the mention of his name.

Everything was going well for Lek until, one day, the king sent for him to kill a crocodile that lived in the river close to his village. "This crocodile especially enjoys eating little boys and girls," said the king gravely. "He eats at least one for dinner every day. I want you to kill this ugly creature and bring it to me."

Of course, Lek shook at the thought of facing a crocodile large enough to eat children, but he could not refuse the king's order. After all, it was Lek's duty as Hon Mee Chong Ra-Ang to protect the people and to serve the king.

The king gave Lek a boat and the assistance of six men armed with rifles. "Kill that crocodile!" everyone cheered as they departed the very next day.

As the boat floated down the fast-flowing, murky river, Lek was very scared. If the boat sank, he would drown because he couldn't swim, or the crocodile would eat him up, or both. Every floating log looked to him like a crocodile and made him jump from his seat. He groaned and moaned, dreading the confrontation.

Suddenly, all six men stopped paddling at once. Within seconds they had their rifles cocked and aimed at a crocodile that was bigger than their boat! There it was on the river's edge, just meters away, sliding down the mud embankment. Lek's hair immediately stood up on end at the sight of it.

The crocodile opened its jaws, and when Lek saw its jagged teeth, he felt all his blood draining out of him. His knees shook so violently that they knocked against each other. His legs finally gave way and he dropped, slouching at the back of the boat and mumbling to himself, "I can be brave. I *am* brave."

A series of powerful blasts went off in quick succession. He covered his ears, trying desperately to drown out the shattering explosions that made his insides shake. He felt a sharp pain in his stomach.

When the gunfire finally stopped, he lifted his head and saw that the small army of men had killed the crocodile.

"The crocodile is dead!" cried the six men.

Hearing that, Lek quickly leaped to his feet and put on a brave face. "What have you done?" he cried. "The king ordered me to kill the crocodile. You heard his orders and you have disobeyed the king! I was not able to do my duty—you have robbed me off my honors," Lek said, raising his voice even more.

The men looked at one another with puzzled expressions. Then, one by one, they set down their weapons.

"When the king hears about this, he will be so angry. You cannot imagine what he will do to you! In this country, everyone must obey the king," Lek told them.

The six men looked very sorry and hung their heads in shame. Lek turned his back on them, pretending to be angry, and listened in as they spoke to one another in panicked voices. Finally, one of them stepped forward. He bowed to Lek and asked for permission to speak.

"You may speak," he said, looking down his nose at the man.

"We have a plan, Honorable One," the man said. "We know you would have killed the crocodile if we had not. We will say that you killed it. This way, you can keep your honors and the king will be happy that you carried out his orders to slay the crocodile."

Lek thought carefully. "I will tell the king that I could not have killed it without the help of six brave men," he replied. With that, everyone was happy.

By the time they arrived at the palace, there was a huge crowd waiting to hear about the exciting adventure. When the people saw Lek standing proudly at the prow of the boat, they began cheering.

Lek held up his hands dramatically until the crowd fell silent. "The crocodile is dead!" he declared. "Our boys and girls are now safe from harm."

The king was so grateful to Lek that he gave him twenty-four rubies, twelve sapphires, two glittering diamonds, and two perfect green emeralds. More important, however, was Lek's new title. The king announced in a royal ceremony that Lek would be called Hon Mee Chong Ra-Ang Wang Chorake, which meant Brave Bear-, Snake-, and Crocodile-Killer. No one in the kingdom had a grander title.

Soon after the great event, Lek went to visit his loyal wife, who still looked after their small rice paddy. After he told her everything, she seemed pleased. "People everywhere are saying that you are fearless," she said. "Some even think you have magical powers to slay all these fierce animals." She squeezed his hand in hers and looked into his eyes. "Maybe you do have some kind of power. One day, you might just be king," she said, smiling.

Hearing this made Lek think. The bears no longer bothered anyone and remained in the forest, the snakes did not come anywhere near the palace, and the crocodiles no longer ate boys and girls. Why, it seemed to Lek that the kingdom was very safe and quiet. He was glad that he helped to cause this peace.

Lek spent the whole night in deep thought until the the crow of the rooster reminded him that it was time to return to the palace.

Back at the palace, Lek rested his head on a silk pillow, still deep in thought. A court musician tapped out soothing rhythms on a snakeskin-covered drum.

Suddenly a messenger burst into the room and said, "Come quickly! The king needs you!"

Lek raced down the corridors and fell to the floor before the king. "I have declared a state of national emergency!" the king announced, looking troubled. "The neighboring kingdom is planning an attack upon us. Hon Mee, I am appointing you commander in chief of our royal army. I know you will lead us to victory."

Lek did not dare look up. If he did, the king might see how frightened he was.

"If you succeed in driving this enemy from our borders," said the king, "I will give you half my kingdom."

"Your Highness, I will drive these attackers from our country!" Lek's reply was bold, but he did not feel so bold. How could he ever solve this problem? *I will try to spy on the enemy and find out more before I take my next step,* Lek decided.

That evening, he crept through the forest to the enemy camp, again whispering to himself, "I can be brave. I *am* brave." Quietly, he climbed up a tall tree and stretched himself out on one of its limbs so that he could listen in on the enemies. He saw a small group of men discussing their battle plans.

"Defeating the entire army of Siam would not be a problem if only the great warrior Hon Mee Chong Ra-Ang Wang Chorake were not leading it," he heard one of the officials say. Lek was all charged up when he heard the words *great warrior.* For once he felt really brave and strong, even powerful.

At that moment, the branch he was hanging on began to crackle. Then, with a loud crack and a great swooshing thud, Lek tumbled out of the tree and somehow landed on his feet, face-to-face with one of the soldiers.

For a split second, Lek was paralyzed with shock, and so was everyone else around him. Lek couldn't move. He just stood there with his eyes and mouth wide open, staring at his enemy, without a single weapon on him.

The men around him grabbed their guns. Still not moving, Lek listened breathlessly to the sound of each weapon being cocked and readied for firing.

Then, suddenly, he thought of what Ying said and knew exactly what to do.

"I am Hon Mee Chong Ra-Ang Wang Chorake!" he said in his deepest, lowest voice. "Come and get me if you dare! But be warned. I have the power to turn you into stone with just one blink of my eye."

Terrified, each man dropped his weapon and tore off into the forest. Lek's reputation as the greatest warrior of all time was enough to scare the enemy away. Nobody dared challenge him.

Soon after, the enemies left the borders and there was peace again in the country. The king sent for Lek and said, "Hon Mee, you have succeeded in driving our enemies away, and you shall have half my kingdom. When I die, you will be my successor."

The next year, just that happened. The king died and Lek became ruler of the land. The very first thing Lek did was fetch his wife, who had faithfully stood by him. He returned to their village mounted on a royal elephant, just as he had once dreamed he would.

"You are indeed blessed, my husband," Ying said to him adoringly.

"Yes, that is true. I am very blessed," said Lek, his eyes twinkling. "In all the world, I could only want one more thing: swimming lessons!"

From then on, Hon Mee Chong Ra-Ang Wang Chorake ruled wisely and well, thanks to the bravery he had learned while doing things he was sure he could not do.

Glossary

Kancil (pronounced kan-chill) is the Malay name of the lesser mousedeer. A native of Southeast Asia, it is the world smallest hoofed mammals; measuring no more than 50 cm long and weighing only 2 kg. This hornless deer-like animal is often featured as the smartest animal and a quick thinker in Malaysian and Indonesian folktales.

Kobito (pronounced ko-bi-to) literally means "little people" in Japanese. In the story of this book, it refers to the imaginary little men and women with special power who help kind people.

Manju is a traditional Japanese steamed sweet cake made from flour.

Tamaraw is a small wild buffalo, weighing about 300 kg (660 lbs). Also called the dwarf buffalo, it is found only in Mindoro, Philippines. With less than 300 of them left in the wild today, tamaraw is one of the rarest land animals around.

Talisay tree is known as the Sea Almond Tree outside the Philippines. A colorful tree used to grow wild on sandy shores in Southeast Asia, it is now commonly cultivated as a popular wayside tree for its beautiful pagoda shape which provide fantastic shade.

Tepee (pronounced tee-pee) is a triangular tent used by American Indians. In the Philippines, it refers to a triangular roost where the roosters rest on.